DOMINION

ALSO BY MONALISA FOSTER

Stand-alone works in the **Ravages of Honor** universe:

Novels

Ravages of Honor: Conquest

Ravages of Honor: Ascension

Novellas

Dominion

Enemy Beloved

Featherlight

Short Story

Bonds of Love and Duty

—Short Fiction—

Pretending to Sleep: A Communism Survivor's Short Story

The Dark Side of the Sun

The Heretic

Catching the Dark

Bellona's Gift

Promethea Invicta: A Novella

Cooper

Collective Responsibility

The Cerberus Project

Good of the Many (forthcoming)

Resilience (forthcoming)

—Non-fiction—

Rejection 101: A Writer's Guide

DOMINION

A RAVAGES OF HONOR NOVELLA

MONALISA FOSTER

For all who serve.

TRANSIT POINT

Galeron approached the phase-shift transit-point, a "surface" in space not unlike the "disk" created by two soap bubbles where they touched.

Nothing on his instruments suggested anything but a stable transit-point, located exactly where it was supposed to be. Still, he hesitated, holding back from taking his fighter-craft through.

Holographic displays sprouted from the semi-circular panel that wrapped around him. Data streams told him that the minor damage his ship had taken was healing as expected.

A snapshot, taken an hour ago, of his prey—another fighter outclassed by his own at least once over—floated within the hologram, the image showing most of its stern.

The longer Galeron waited, the greater the chance that he would lose his prey's trail. Yet, here he was, lurking.

He sank back into the yielding grip of his pilot's chair, and ran his thumb along the smooth, pearlescent surface of the armrest. The ship's smooth interior was like the inside of an egg-shell, ready to sprout additional controls and interfaces as needed. They remained dormant as clean, sanitized air—its movement the only motion in the stillness— filled his nostrils, then his lungs.

Teirani Tutori, former sister-in-arms, now vassal of an enemy House, had fled before him. According to his ship's data, Gota-Dai, the system on the other side, had six other known transit-points. And if Teirani took any one of them, she'd disappear.

Galeron's instruments could only detect gravitic waves from her fighter for a limited time. A time he was wasting here, hesitating. It wasn't cowardice. Nor sentiment.

It was his ardent desire to catch and defeat her.

It was written into his nature, his *donai* genetic code, as much as the almost-human appearance, the layered irises that gave him augmented vision. The enhanced hearing, strength and agility. The ability to heal. The symbiosis with his nanites.

All the things that made him more than human, made him, *donai*.

His hand tightened on the throttle without moving it. He ordered the ship to prepare a dozen message drones and load them with telemetry.

"My lord, I am in pursuit of House Dynadin's *donai*," he added to the message. "If this is where the information we seek has been hidden, I will send confirmation."

He couldn't be any more specific. Should any other House capture one of the drones before they made it back, details would betray House Cadarn's goals. He ordered the ship to calculate a dozen random routes to Lord Cadarn's three most likely locations.

The routes appeared on the holographic display, a jumble of strings branching out from his position, twisting and corkscrewing not through physical space, but through the extra-dimensional space of the phase-shift transit system. Should one of the drones make it—and he had no expectation that more than one would—House Cadarn would sent help.

He verified that the telemetry and report had been loaded, powered up the drones, and deployed them with full stealth.

"All drones are away," the ship confirmed.

He pushed the throttle forward. His fighter's prow pierced the transit-point, disappearing into a disk barely large enough to accommodate small ships like his and that of his prey.

There was no disorientation, no indication at all that he'd just traveled thousands of lightyears. There was, in fact, no change in momentum at all. He simply was someplace else, someplace far outside House Cadarn's territory, away from help of any kind, for at least as long as it took the drones to reach their destination and for his liege lord to dispatch reinforcements, assuming all went as planned.

The Gota-Dai system was unclaimed. And no wonder. A single planet, the fourth, was suitable for human life.

The footprints left by Teirani's gravitic engines were aimed towards that world. Assuming she hadn't slingshotted around it, engines off, leaving no footprints, his destination was clear.

Galeron pulled up all the data his ship had on Gota-Dai. No orbital platforms, no communication arrays or relays, nothing to indicate the presence of the Ryhma—the human faction that had created the *donai*, used them to destroy their enemies, and then ordered them to self-destruct.

Supposedly, Ryhman survivors had scattered and set up hundreds of primitive seed colonies, hoping to escape the attentions of the *donai* and the chaos that had resulted from their rebellion.

Several *donai* Houses were now actively seeking out these seed colonies, determined to subjugate all humans before they could rise to power again. Some had more aggressive solutions—wiping out humans en masse, or only allowing the most docile amongst them to survive and taking them as chattel.

The sovereign of House Cadarn seemed to be of two minds, sometimes acting benevolently, other times showing no mercy. Galeron could see no pattern in his reasoning, and he'd never been in a position to demand an explanation, or be offered one.

Once the planet's gravity well became dominant, Teirani's footprints vanished. There were no other planets that she or her wounded ship could survive on, no gas giants to hide in while her ship healed. And if she'd fled through the transit-points, the game was lost.

He approached the fourth planet. A few orbits told him what he needed to know. Her ship had made a crash landing on one of the lesser continents.

It would've made more sense for her wounded ship to go through a transit point than attempt an atmospheric re-entry in its condition. Teirani had chosen to approach this system for a reason—because it certainly wasn't the shortest, fastest, or safest route to anywhere, by any stretch of the imagination.

Every *donai* House was after two things—revenge on any Ryhman survivors and their creators' knowledge.

2

BOG

*A*ny landing you could walk—or crawl—away from, was a good one.

Teirani's crab-crawl through the nighttime bog was lit by a section of burning fuselage. The blaze was keeping the larger predators at bay, at least for the time being. They lurked outside the circle of light, their bodies glowing in her enhanced vision, as they prowled back and forth, occasionally communicating with each other via sub-sonic bursts that sounded like feedback booms.

It was her right arm that was the problem.

It was broken, in at least two places, and her accelerated healing had already started knitting the bones together before she'd regained consciousness and had a chance to realign them. It was never a pleasant process, setting one's own breaks, but they all knew how to do it.

It was part of their training, part of being *donai*.

Her leg was the other problem. Not a bone break, but the tendons and muscles of her left calf had been eaten by something. It's what had pulled her back to painful consciousness, but the creature feasting on her had disappeared into the sludge, apparently satisfied with just a taste.

Or maybe she wasn't to its liking.

The bite had spared the bone, but she wasn't going to be able to stand or walk until everything else grew back, which would likely take a few hours by the feel of it—hours she didn't have.

She rolled over to catch her breath. Her survival pack bit into her spine. Cold sludge seeped into and under the suit where her calf had been opened. Her nanites would take care of most micro-organisms, but the feel of it still made her skin crawl.

She patted her left side. Her sword was still there. Her sidearm was a reassuring weight on her right hip. She strained to reach across and draw it from its holster. She raised it, aimed, and fired at the largest of a trio of predators.

The canid-looking thing, about the size of a human, dropped. The others scattered, those sub-sonic bursts cresting to a painful volume.

She laid the gun across her chest, and covered one ear with her hand until the painful sound faded and the creatures retreated. A hot, wet trickle from the unprotected ear told her that the bursts done some damage.

Nothing like more blood to draw whatever else was around here. The death of a thousand cuts may not lead to death, at least not for a *donai*, but it was sure going to make this mission … challenging.

It better be worth it.

Straining, she reholstered her gun. She'd have to find some way to get that holster detached and positioned across her belly, but not while she was crawling. And first, she had to get as far away from her ship as possible.

A streak of light raced across the moonless sky. Galeron's ship, no doubt. And maybe other House Cadarn ships to follow.

She drew her mangled arm into the diagonal seal that crossed the front of her flight suit. Pain spotted her vision as she tugged the seals tight enough to hold the useless, throbbing arm in place. She rolled over, wincing at the flood of cold sludge now seeping across her chest and down her belly. She crawled.

Push with the right leg. Brace with the left elbow. Adjust the pack.

The information Galeron and his sovereign were after existed only in one place—her head. Of this she had made sure. Nothing remained in the ship's logs. Nothing to give away the location of the Ark, the sanctuary where the Ryhmans had hidden the genetic engineering secrets that had allowed them to create the *donai.*

Right leg. Left elbow.

Watery sludge flowed around her, giving way. She cursed. Swimming was not an option. Not in this condition.

The shoreline was in sight. Small creatures hopped on paired, reed-like legs with reversed knee joints. They dipped their snouts into the brackish water. She veered off to the left where the flow of decaying vegetation indicated shallower water.

She wasn't far from the Ark. Maybe a few days on foot. Even injured, she could make it, as long as she didn't make some phenomenally stupid mistake that got her head crushed, or knocked her out long enough for the locals to make a meal out of her.

This is why we fight in packs.

Push with the right leg. Brace with the left elbow.

She anchored the toes of her left boot into the muck and gave it just a little push to test its progress. The stab of pain bolted up her leg and into her hip. No time to curl into the fetal position and whimper.

Instead, she prayed that one of the message drones that she'd dispatched through Gota-Dai's transit-points would make it into House Dynadin's hands as quickly as the ship's intelligence had estimated. She was still looking at a week alone, without help, without pack mates. It was of little comfort that Galeron's communiques were similarly limited.

It would be just the two of them. At least for awhile.

Damn. Why did it have to be him? Of all of House Cadarn's *donai,* why did it have to be *him*?

Right leg. Left elbow. Over and over again. Like a machine. A wounded one, with grinding gears and leaking fluids, mindless in its pursuit of a simple goal.

Just one more cycle of whatever it took to inch forward. And nothing else. Then another cycle.

The humans should've made the *donai* as machines, rather than in their own image. With a machine, you could swap out damaged parts. You didn't have to worry about machines that refused or questioned or doubted orders.

Right leg. Left elbow.

The night air stirred. Chirps and calls reappeared. Her ear must've healed. Another design flaw. She'd rather have the nanites concentrate on healing her leg. She pushed her left boot into the muck again. It wasn't blindingly painful.

No urge to go fetal. No urge to whimper. But still not enough. Soon though. Soon.

Please, let it be soon.

One final push. One final pull, and she was ashore.

She released the survival pack's catches and eased it off her good shoulder, then released the buckle at her waist. She rolled, like a turtle casting off its shell, easing the sword off her side so she could sit up.

Slowly, carefully, she repositioned the knife sheath at the small of her back so it'd be easier to draw left-handed. It strained and pulled at already taxed muscles, but it had to be done. The holster was easier. It detached and she remounted it over her belly-button. With any luck there would be no more crawling in her future.

Dawn broke as Gota-Dai sent rose-gold light through the distant tree line. The wind shifted.

She smelled Galeron before she saw him.

Teirani pushed herself up, placing weight on her injured leg, drawing her gun, and pointing it at Galeron as he emerged from the trees lining the shore.

His flight suit shifted colors to blend into the changing background as he approached. There was a smirk on his face. The light caught the obsidian thickness of his neatly trimmed beard, the mahogany skin of his scalp. He moved with *donai* speed, and was behind her before she could squeeze the trigger.

And then her sidearm was out of her reach, torn from her grasp, and there was a knife at her throat, and his breath in her ear.

"Hesitation, from you, Teirani? I wouldn't have believed it, had I not seen it."

3

TERMS

he pale gold of Teirani's short flaxen hair was green from all
the sludge.

She looked up at Galeron, throat exposed, pulse pounding, pain and
fear scenting the crisp morning air around them. Every inch on her
ivory skin was covered in a thick layer of decaying vegetation and oily
muck.

Her gold and amber gaze met his and her face became devoid of
emotion as she donned that same mask they all learned to wear.

"Who's the one hesitating now?" she asked, her tone as cold and
fragile as the crystals of a fresh frost.

"You have information I want," he said. "It is not the same."

"And you mean to tear it out of me?"

He slid the knife up her throat, used it to lift her chin higher with
the flat of the blade.

"If need be," he said, and meant it. "That's the problem with our
kind, isn't it? We don't die like a human would. We heal."

She shifted her weight but he caught her hand before it could go for
the knife at her back. He spun her, knocking the blade out of her grasp.
She fell back on the sandy soil, and backed away from him, scooting

back on one elbow and one leg, her throat bleeding from the fresh cut his blade had made.

He kicked her sword out of her reach as well, and followed her at a slow, leisurely pace.

"I have a proposition for you," he said. "There's an equal chance that either of our Houses will respond first. I think you're here for a very good reason—one having to do with the Ryhma, perhaps even with our creation. I have the means to help you find what you seek. You have my word. I will not harm you. And my word as well, that should House Dynadin land here first, I will surrender."

"Surrender?" she said, backing up a little more. "You'd offer my liege lord your head?"

Galeron took a deep breath.

She *was* here for something of great importance. Such importance, that sharing in her knowledge would warrant his death.

Whatever doubts he'd had about why she was here were swept away by the pain contorting her face. It fractured that delicate mask for just an instant before reforming. All the things that physical pain had not brought to the surface were brought forth by the idea of his death.

"If that is what your liege lord demands," he said. "Death before dishonor is how we were made."

"Why? Why court death at all?"

"Because the other option is to return to my sovereign empty-handed. At least this way, there's a fifty-fifty chance that I'll return with you as my prisoner, and with your knowledge as my prize."

Her eyes widened, and behind those layered irises, he could almost see the thoughts churning in her mind. She was running the odds, doing her own calculations.

The delicate skin between her eyes tugged into a thoughtful frown.

He'd never forget this image of her, covered in muck, her hair spiked with green sludge, arm uselessly cradled to her chest, unable to stand, so vulnerable, yet undefeated.

Never had she looked more beautiful.

The thought struck him like an invisible force and penetrated his defenses. A sister-in-arms. A comrade. A pack mate. An adversary. A rival. She was or had been all those things.

And beautiful.

She wet her lips, the gesture powering up that invisible probe to stab at his defenses once again.

She'd been injured and healing required certain resources—like food and water. It was thirst, nothing more. And he would offer to quench it, once she agreed. And not a second earlier.

"We work together, like before we chose sides," she said. "Our Houses don't enter into this until one of them makes an appearance."

"And your word, that should House Cadarn land first, you will surrender."

Her fingers clawed into the wet sand beneath her.

"My word of honor as *donai*," she said. "Should House Cadarn land first, I will surrender."

4

CARETAKER

*E*ven with Galeron hefting her survival pack and all the weapons, as well as bearing most of her weight, the pain in her healing calf had outpaced the ache in her arm a hill or two ago.

Mostly, her injured arm had been numb, which was never a good sign. Just because the nanites could repair tissue, didn't mean that the repaired tissue would function properly. Something must be awry. Misaligned nerves, or tendons, or blood vessels. They were the most likely candidates with a break of this kind.

Sweat poured off her. Her flight suit was crusty and it felt like it was crawling with things. She raised the water bottle to her lips and took another sip.

The world around her did a little spin, and then she was cradled across Galeron's arms.

She used her left arm to push against his chest. He gave her a little bounce and resettled her in his embrace.

"Do that again, and I'll drop you on your ass," he said. "You can crawl after me the rest of the way."

And he'd do it. His tone left no doubt of that.

"How much further?" she asked.

"Just over that hill," he said, gesturing with his chin. "My ship is there, and there's a river. Now, put your arm around my neck and hold on."

No sooner had she done so, that he moved.

The forest canopy above was a blur. He wasn't moving at full speed, but at a pace to keep from jostling her too badly.

Sweat ran down his face and neck, sending pheromones her way in tiny snippets before the wind snatched them away.

She shook her head to clear it, pulling away from his chest without loosening her grip around his neck. His sweat mixed with her own, an odd tingling sensation that was, no doubt, a result of her weakened state.

The promise of a river meant a bath, or at least a chance to clean up. If it was the same river she'd been aiming for, the one that became a waterfall, leading into a valley, then they were close to the Ark.

The human she'd obtained the information from—a member of the hated Ryhma—had confessed to the Ark's existence during her dying days. Not out of fear, or pain, although Teirani had been sent to obtain that information by whatever means was necessary.

No, the old woman's words were driven by a mixture of dementia and guilt.

A caretaker, she'd called herself. At one point, she'd reached out, hand trembling, her papery skin so thin it was almost translucent, and touched Teirani's cheek and said, *You were a pretty little girl once. I held you and nursed you and tucked you into bed. Do you remember?*

Teirani had not.

It was possible. Those early childhood memories were vague. Her memories began much later, when she'd started training, around six or so.

But *donai* children didn't have mothers. At least not what humans thought of as mothers. They were not born, but created. First in test tubes, then in gestation tanks.

If the frail old woman—Avyanna, she'd called herself—had been her caretaker, Teirani didn't recognize her, didn't feel any sort of connection at all.

In her more lucid moments, Avyanna had looked at her as if she were a stranger. And in her not-so-lucid ones, she'd called her Daughter. And when Teirani had called her Mother, the old woman had wept openly, with a full dose of misery and guilt.

It was then she spoke of the Ark, of the children abandoned within it. She hadn't wanted to leave them, but the Ryhman leaders had not given her a choice. They'd made all the caretakers board a ship and then scattered them throughout the universe, far and wide, like seeds set on winds that swept across barren soil.

Some had been killed for refusing to go. Others for speaking up.

Avyanna had been afraid. She'd confessed her fear, crying fat tears into Teirani's hands, kissing them, begging forgiveness.

Forgiveness for what? Teirani had asked.

For abandoning the children. They were alive, Avyanna had whispered, her gaze darting as if she expected the ghost of some Ryhman leader to appear out of thin air and strike her down. Her heart rate had spiked, sending all the bio-monitors screeching, and bringing the prison staff to the cell.

It had taken days of waiting, cajoling, playing the alternating roles of stranger and imaginary daughter, but then Avyanna had finally revealed, not only the Ark's location, but the vastness of the treasure it contained: thousands of *donai* embryos, the most advanced versions the Ryhma had created; and alongside those, in stasis, thousands more in advanced gestation.

And one more thing, or at least, so Teirani had understood, the real prize—the means by which to make more *donai* so that her sub-species wouldn't be condemned to extinction. The *donai* were long-lived— their nanites and enhancements made them so.

But they were infertile by design.

They were genetic dead ends.

And nothing more.

5

MUSCLE AND BONE

Galeron slowed as he crested the last hill. His ship waited on the flatlands on the other side of the river.

Stealthed, it shimmered like the mirage of a giant egg. It was a fitting way to look at it. Its design had always reminded him of a bird of prey—a raptor of some kind, designed to hunt and kill, to tear its prey to shreds and rule the skies.

Teirani had gone very still in his arms. Her breathing had slowed as well, and a miasma of pain floated around her like a blanket, one he very much wanted to free her from.

It was, in many ways, the wrong reaction. A rival House's vassal, he should be thinking of ways to leverage that pain in his favor, not ease it.

"You're thinking deep thoughts," he said as he crossed the river via a silt bed.

He slowed again. He was in no hurry to set her down, let her out of his arms.

"Am I?" Teirani asked. "How can you tell?"

"You always get this line between your brows," he said, as he stepped onto the riverbank.

"Do I?"

He grunted as he lowered her. She put her healthy leg down and he helped her stand, but when she shifted her weight onto her damaged leg, her knees buckled. He caught her.

She gave him a grateful grin, and lowered herself to the ground.

He dropped the pack, and knelt beside her, turning her leg gently. She winced, but she held still, allowing him to get a better look.

"Another day, at least," he said. "If you stay off of it."

She aimed a raised brow at him. "I don't suppose you have something useful in that ship of yours."

"Food. Weapons."

"I'll take some of both," she said and smiled.

He lifted his head to the sky. "Short days here. Fire first. Then I'm going to rebreak your arm. Save the food for after. You're going to need it."

He built her a fire, a large one that no passing ship would miss and no predator would dare approach.

Her eyes were glassy with pain by the time he was done. He rummaged through her pack until he found what he was looking for: her field kit's brace and wrapping.

"You ready?" he asked.

She nodded and shifted slightly away from him, even as she opened up the seal of her flight suit. Her small breasts were covered in muck.

He wrapped his hand around her wrist and supported her elbow with the other, moving the arm with deliberate slowness. The full spectrum of his enhanced vision, told him it was a mess. He'd not trained as a medic, but even he could tell that there was compromised blood flow and the sparks given off by nerve impulses no longer reached her fingers.

"I need to remove the sleeve," he said.

She nodded, glassy-eyed and distant.

He used the knife to bare her arm, identified two misaligned breaks, and a third break so severe that bone jutted up against the skin. If she'd been human, the bone would've pierced the skin, but their creators had made their skin hardier than their bones. In most instances the design served them well, the skin yielding only to the nanometer edges of *donai* swords and knives.

Teirani bit her lip and looked away.

He broke and realigned the misaligned bones that had healed. She didn't scream until he moved the third full fracture into place. Nerve impulses throbbed and flared like beacons in his augmented vision confirming that the sharp edges of those breaks were slicing through newly-healed muscles and tendons, and severing misrouted nerves.

He braced and wrapped the arm and then pulled her into his embrace, cursing all of humanity.

A *donai's* nanites rendered inert anything that might alleviate pain. It was a blessing in that it made them immune to incapacitation via drugs or gasses. It was a curse as well. The speed with which they healed mostly made up for it.

Mostly, but not today.

Wet drops landed on the arm he'd wrapped across her collarbone. They hit his skin as though they were fire, scorching their way down. A cloud of pain-scent had settled over them. It soured in his throat, but he held her for far longer than he should have.

She was asleep and the prudent thing to do would be to wake and feed her. The healing process was energy-intensive, and the nanites would cannibalize her own uninjured tissues if necessary. She'd be weak when she woke.

If she'd been his pack mate, he'd have watched over her, made sure she slept, made her sip water, and had plenty of sustenance when she woke. He wouldn't take advantage of her weakness.

But a weak rival *was* preferable to a strong one.

She mumbled as he laid her down on her side. He emptied the survival pack, set aside the fatigues, laid out the rations, then set her atop the pack.

He cut her out of the flight suit, and tossed the bloodied scraps into the fire. A putrid stench rose from the spitting, hissing flames. She stirred, mumbled again, turned away from the stench, but didn't wake.

Galeron stripped her bare and washed her, using the undershirt of her spare fatigues for a rag. He ran the dripping wet rag over every inch of her, drenching her hair until it was dark gold and no trace of green remained. He touched her only when necessary, just as he would do for any other *donai*.

He picked off the minuscule leech-like organisms attached to the exposed muscle of her injured calf. The leeches were dead—her nanites had killed them—but the piercing suckers kept them anchored to her flesh. He tossed them into the fire, and wrapped her healing calf as well.

When he used his visual augmentations to check for other injuries, he lingered. Cleaning her up had been like peeling a chrysalis to find a beautiful creature dormant within. The definition of her muscles, the smoothness of her skin—strength wrapped in satin. It was the only way to describe her.

And not a way one should describe, or think of, a sister-in-arms.

Or a rival.

6

A RACE

Teirani woke to the scent of grilling meat. She was clean,
dressed, her injured arm set and cradled in a sling tied
across her chest.

She'd have done the same for Galeron. But she wasn't sure she'd
have put his sword, knife, and sidearm within easy reach, as he'd done.
She'd been genetically engineered to be a match for any male *donai* of
comparable size. In this, they were different from humans.

But size still mattered.

He was taller, almost by a head. And he still outweighed her. By at
least half. From the sparring matches of their youth, she knew she had
better reflexes and could outrun him.

Her injured arm wasn't as much of an issue either—every *donai*
was proficient using either side, whether sword, knife, or sidearm. Or
any other weapon for that matter.

With her arm set and healing properly now, giving her back her
weapons meant he'd surrendered any leverage he might have had over
her. Well, he *had* given her his word and accepted hers in return.

Should House Dynadin's forces arrive first, her liege lord would
demand Galeron's head without hesitation. Not just because by then

Galeron would know about the Ark, but because the two of them had spent time in isolation.

It wouldn't be the first time Dynadin had demanded that one of his vassals demonstrate their loyalty by taking a rival's life. A trembling shudder passed through her, shaking her to her core.

Galeron sat across from her, munching on a hunk of meat, his golden eyes glowing at her like embers. Was he too weighing the value of his honor? And hers? The weapons were a sign of trust. Or dominance. Him, granting permission.

Favoring her injured arm, she sat up and pulled at her left pant leg. Slowly, she undid the wrapping. Her muscle had grown back and skin was forming over the wound. She tested it by pointing her toes, flexing her foot. There was an ache and weakness. It would be at least a few days before the muscle would regain its former strength.

So, outrunning him was not an option, at least for now.

Galeron rose and came forward with a plate full of meat and a canteen.

"Thank you," she said as she accepted them.

He must have been giving her water because she wasn't nearly as thirsty as she should've been, but she was ravenously hungry. By the look of it, he'd gone out and killed several animals. There was plenty for both of them without needing to dip into survival rations.

They ate in silence under a dark, cloudless sky sprinkled with naked, unfamiliar stars.

"Why?" she asked after her belly was full to almost painful.

He quirked a dark eyebrow at her, his lip tilting up at the same time in a half-smile.

"Why what?"

She aimed her gaze at the weapons and then leveled it back at him.

"Are you surrendering them to me?" he asked.

"No." It rushed out with a raise in pitch that made her cringe.

"Well, if it comes to it, I'll take them in honorable combat, Teirani. Until then, they remain yours."

He resumed eating, elbows propped casually on both knees. He'd changed into fatigues as well, sleeves and pant legs turned up into cuffs, his feet bare, his toes digging into the sand.

"Should House Cadarn land, what will your sovereign demand of me?" she asked.

"A share in whatever we find here."

"And my head?"

He stopped chewing, and wiped his mouth with his hand. "Probably not your head. Maybe ransom … or you could request amnesty."

"I will not betray my House."

Amnesty was another word for betrayal. Only her liege lord could release her from her oath of fealty, and any lord willing to accept her fealty after she'd betrayed another, was an utter, despicable fool. Lord Cadarn had a reputation for being many things, but not a fool.

"We agreed to set aside House politics, House loyalties," he said, "until the mission was over, did we not?"

"We did." She gave him a gracious tilt of agreement.

"In the morning," she added, "we should head downriver."

"How far do we need to go?"

"A day's march. Maybe two," she said, rubbing at her calf. At a good run, they could be there by morning.

"There is room in my fighter for you. It'd be easier to fly there."

"There may be automated defenses," she said. "I only have codes for entry via a hidden service tunnel."

"My sensors showed no power sources, nothing to indicate automated defenses or anything that might pose a threat. There is no Ryhman presence here, no sign that there ever was."

She took a deep breath. Trust. She needed to trust. He needed to know the scope, the scale of the danger in which he'd chosen to share.

"It's a Ryhman Ark," she said. "One called, *Dominion*."

He choked and pounded his chest to clear it, then took a long pull from his canteen.

"Are you certain?" he asked.

"Certain enough to have risked my life coming here alone instead of taking the information to my House first."

His eyes widened. "Why?"

"Because I'm not the only one who knows," she said.

In one of her more lucid moments, Avyanna had told her that she was not the first to come for her secrets. Only that she hoped that Teirani would be the last.

And then with a blink of an eye, she'd regressed to being a caretaker, bony fingers playing with Teirani's short hair. *Such cute little ears*, she'd said. *You should let your hair grow out, Daughter, so I can braid it for you again.*

"So it's a race against time," Galeron said.

"We must also be cautious. Should we approach by air, trigger their defenses, the contents of the Ark will be destroyed."

"Contents," he said, enunciating. "How many *donai* lives are we talking about, Teirani?"

"Thousands. Maybe hundreds of thousands."

"That's more *donai* than are alive now."

"And the means to make more," she added in a whisper.

He rushed forward, falling to his knees in front of her. He placed his hands on her shoulders, his gaze searching her face with hungry desperation.

"What means?" he asked, his fingers digging into her flesh until she winced.

Teirani wet her lips, hesitating.

"I'm not quite sure," she said.

He gave her a sharp look.

"It's true," she said, pushing him away. "My source said many things, some of which made no sense at all."

He let her go and sat back on his heels, running his hand over his scalp.

"Who else knows?"

"House Kabrin."

7

CLIFF

There was no way Galeron was going to allow House Kabrin
to take the Ark. It would give them too much power.
Perhaps even enough to form an empire. He darted about, breaking
camp as Teirani argued at him about the need to wait until morning, her
voice rising, her words turning from reason to pleading and back again.

"I'll carry you if need be," he said.

"You can't carry me, and our weapons, and our supplies."

"You've been out for the better part of three local days. Kabrin's
agent may have chosen to report in first, but I doubt they'll bide their
time."

She swore and pulled on her boots.

He restocked her pack with fresh supplies and they headed downriver. As Gota-Dai rose behind them, she moved at a good clip for
someone whose leg was still healing and not up to full strength.

The susurrations of a waterfall drifted their way and when they
reached the cliff, it was he who insisted on a rest-stop. She didn't argue,
betraying her fatigue. She ate, looking up to search the sky with
worried eyes.

"Do you remember your caretaker?" she asked between bites.

"Bits and pieces," he said as he took a look down the cliffside. A white cloud rose off jagged boulders. It was a sheer drop. How did she intend to get down there?

"What bits and pieces?" She stood and joined him, her gaze sweeping over the valley below and the terrain on the other side of the river.

The valley was cut deep and wide but the trees down there couldn't be more than a few decades old. There was nothing in the topography to indicate any technology had been used to create or alter it. It's what he would have expected of the Ryhmans.

"She had skin like yours," he said. "And blue eyes. They crinkled when she laughed. She liked to sing."

"Do you remember her name?"

"No."

He remembered everything since he was six with absolute clarity. Everything before was murky, and getting murkier with time.

"Why?" he asked.

"Do you think they loved us?"

"Our caretakers?" He scratched at his beard. That drop was too sheer, the boulders below too jagged. They could survive it, but it was too much of a risk. A smashed-in skull was all it would take. Their nanites couldn't heal their brains.

"It's down there," Teirani said, pointing to the cliff face and a narrow ledge that led downward toward the valley floor.

He gave her a skeptical look, resting his gaze on her injured arm.

"It's not that far," she said. "I can do it."

"And if you fall, I'll be without the means to go any farther. No."

"I'll give you the codes. Just bury me. I'd rather not be food."

"No," he said. "You, on my back."

"Fine. Give me your sword."

He handed it over.

She worked efficiently, securing the swords through cinches built into the pack, then hefting it to one shoulder.

He clicked the waist strap closed for her.

"Turn around," she said.

He gave her his back.

"If you drop me," she said, as she climbed onto his back, "I'll haunt you for the rest of your life."

He smiled as her forearm clamped against his chest and her legs tightened around him.

He edged onto the ledge, making sure his footing was stable.

"My mother told me she loved me," he said plunging his fingers into the stone. It gave way, crumbling in his grip. The handholds he made now would make the trek back far easier.

"You called her 'mother'?" she asked.

He grunted. Slid. Punched through the rock.

With each step and slide, the rock was getting denser. His fingers were taking some damage. Even with the nanites rallying to make repairs, he slowed. It would do them no good if blood-slicked tissue made him lose his grip.

"What else do you remember?" she asked a few steps later.

"Her hair was like yours too," he said as the ledge narrowed.

It forced him to pull in tight against the rocks, press his hips—and the legs wrapped around them—into the wall. Her grip on him never wavered, not even as wind pulled at them. His groin stirred awake with unreasonable demands, like how much better it would be to have her legs wrapped around him the other way.

"How much farther?" he asked.

"Just a few steps. I think."

The ledge was widening, but the vegetation clinging to the rock face was thickening. The vines had thick stems covered in sharp spikes that had bored into the rock, but seemed to be rooted far above. He carved out a deep handhold, tested its integrity, and dug in.

"Did she braid her hair?" Teirani asked.

"Yes," he said as he gave one of the thicker vines a good tug. It gave way, separating from the rock face above. Tiny bits of debris and vegetation rained down on them. He shook the debris out of his eyes as his fingers probed for another vine.

Tug. Separation. Debris. Repeat.

Behind the fifth vine, there was only empty space. The veil of vegetation was hiding an opening. He edged closer, tucking them under the veil. The vine's spikes scraped across his scalp, like teasing fingers tipped with sharp nails.

Teirani tucked her head into his neck, her breath a gentle caress that pebbled his skin. Her fingers had a death's grip on his shirt and the sharpness of *her* nails dug into the muscles of his chest in hopeless parody of what his body wanted—her nails digging into his back.

His next slide brought them into the tunnel. He went to one knee, and drew his sidearm as Teirani slid off his back and did the same. Behind them, the vines were like a thick curtain, blocking out most of Gota-Dai's light.

The tunnel was smooth, bored out by controlled plasma bursts. He'd wanted signs of Ryhman tech and here it was. Echoes of dripping water bounced off the smooth, glasslike surface. It reminded him of a battleship's launch tubes. It might even be a battleship launch tube, for all he knew. Or its ground-based equivalent.

"Forward?" he asked.

"Always."

8

ARK

Teirani strapped her sword onto her right side, and took point. This was no service tunnel. Avyanna had either been wrong or had misspoken. Or she'd brought them to the wrong place.

She heard Galeron lift the pack and move behind her. There was nothing in the dark tunnel except cracks that dripped water. No intruding vegetation, and none of the insects or small animals one would expect to make such a convenient refuge into a home. There were no betraying power sources for defenses of any kind, not even sensors.

She sped up, moving as fast as her protesting calf allowed. Eventually, she stopped to give it a chance to rest and glanced behind her. The opening appeared to be half its original size. The darkness at the other end seemed to go on and on.

Hours later, when the opening was a mere pinprick, the tunnel split into three. She hunched over, rested her hand on her knee, and caught her breath.

"Teirani," Galeron said, his voice a cautious whisper. "Which way?"

She shook her head and laughed.

"The crazy old woman said there was a hatchway near the split."

Galeron looked around. "I don't see anything."

Neither did she, no matter how much of her enhanced vision she used. "Start feeling around. There has to be something. A seam. A sensor plate."

"Sensor plates need power," he said, but dropped the pack and ran his hands over the right side of the tube.

She did the same, tracing the curving wall on the left.

Unfortunately, he was right. A sensor plate required power. But if there was no power, there was no way to stealth the entryway either.

"Will blasting our way through or drilling set off any countermeasures?" he asked, now on his knees, his hands working patiently.

"Probably."

Avyanna had spoken of terrible traps, her voice shaking with fear, her hands shaking from memories that made her go silent or burst into tears that wouldn't stop, sometimes for hours.

Teirani turned at Galleron's sharp intake of breath. It was followed by a scraping sound and the whir of mechanical gears turned by a counterweight. The narrow entrance opened, revealing another swallowing darkness.

Galeron stood. "No code panel."

"Maybe further in."

He ducked his head and shifted his shoulders to make it through. She followed, breathing in moist air tainted with the decay of vegetation. The hairs on the back of her neck rose.

The only light was a gray murky stillness in the distance.

She broke into a run and was jerked back by Galeron's hand on her shoulder.

She spun, ducking under his grip, and gave him a one-handed shove that made him grunt.

"Don't you dare," she said, shooting him a venomous glare.

He was on edge. She could smell it on him. And so was she.

It was the lack of active defenses. Ryhman tech was well-known for them. Power should be flowing to dormant systems, glowing in their vision.

Something should be happening. And wasn't. It was like being inside an ancient tomb.

Her heart thundered as she sprinted towards the gray light.

She skidded to a halt as she emerged from the tunnel and onto a platform. The cavernous chamber was in the shape of a large hangar, one that would've easily held dozens of larger fighters spaced at least a wingspan apart. It had smooth, glasslike walls like the tunnel from which they'd emerged. The gray light was from a hole in the ceiling, a large one, frilled with vines that corkscrewed all the way to the hangar floor.

Night had fallen.

Insects and birds took flight at their presence, their bodies giving off minuscule heat signatures, as they escaped through the hole. Snake- and lizard-like creatures slithered on the floor below.

She took the steps two at a time and jumped the last few to the hangar floor, landing slightly off balance.

It was an Ark. Of that, there was no doubt.

A massive control station full of dormant consoles, very much like the bridge of a cruiser, was tucked under the platform. It continued outward down the long axis of the hangar. Human skeletons still wearing Ryhman uniforms were sprawled over the consoles, their skulls sporting large holes.

All of the equipment one would expect of an Ark was present— bays and bays of cryogenic units, filled with thousands of test-tubes. Most of them were smashed.

She picked up an intact one. The seal had cracked, the liquid evaporated. Somewhere in the residue at the bottom was a desiccated *donai* embryo. She tucked it to her chest and moved to the next cryo-bay.

Teirani couldn't tell if the power had failed first, or if Gota-Dai IV's animals had done the damage. Their remains, skeletons in various stages of decay littered the ground. By the look of it, once they'd fallen into the Ark, they hadn't been able to find their way back out.

She moved towards a cluster of gestation tanks. Most had been smashed open and were empty. She couldn't decide which was a worse fate? Being eaten before you had a chance to live or drowning in your own waste as the tank failed.

Had they been aware? Had they been in pain? So many of them, snuffed out, before taking their first breath.

Fifteen pods later, she stopped, unable to go on, sinking to her knees, dropping the test-tube and splaying her hand over a tank with a child inside. His face looked as if he were still asleep, his thumb in his mouth, the points of his ears peeking through a thick mop of dark red hair. He was still in death, the fluids around him murky with blood and black chunks.

How long had he been dead? Not nearly as long as the others. Maybe days. Maybe … hours.

Dominion might have once been an Ark.

But it had become a tomb.

9

BATTLE

Galeron inspected the rest of the Ark with meticulous care. The main data core had lost power and parts of it were damaged —something had penetrated the seals and eroded it, but he decoupled the core and stuffed it into the pack.

Perhaps someone with the right tools and training would recover the data. Chances were that anything organic was useless, but he took a few tubes with desiccated embryos as well.

He squatted down in front of Teirani, wiping away her tears with his thumb. As before, it set a spark loose over his skin.

"Can you help me remove the sling, please?" she asked, lifting her gaze to his.

"Are you healed?"

"Not fully, but I'd like it off anyway."

He hesitated for a moment, then helped her out of it. With careful, precise motions, she tested the joints. Pain scented the beads of sweat that appeared at her hairline.

"This is the only intact sample," he said nodding at the red-headed child.

"I know," she said.

She moved like a ghost, a shell of the once vibrant woman she'd been, the light in her eyes fading, as they separated the tank from the pods. She cradled the tank in her arms as Galeron climbed the corkscrewing vines leading to the surface. He took the pack up first, then the tank, then returned for her. She tucked her head into the back of his neck and drenched it with tears.

"Our mission is still a success," he said as they emerged from the hole and he set her down.

She fell to her knees, and ran her hands hesitantly over the tank. He needed to get it into the pack or shroud it in some way. That still face, so peaceful, so still, a parody of life, made his gut wrench—with impotent rage and a visceral need for vengeance—whenever he looked at it.

"We have a salvaged data core," he continued, "the location of the remaining samples, and it looks like there's not much left to interest predators down there. We can return with specialists."

She wrapped her arms around the tank, cradling it, and headed in the general direction of his ship, her steps without vigor. He'd seen that type of walk before. In prisoners being marched to their deaths. She resisted all his attempt to take the tank, first shaking her head, then ignoring him.

When he insisted she rest, she kept marching. He dropped the pack, grabbed her shoulder, and spun her around.

She gave him a defiant look.

"Set it down," he ordered. "Rest."

She set the tank down, lowering it with exquisite care, her hand lingering in a caress.

Then she was at his throat, her blade at his carotid, her eyes ablaze.

"You have no idea what this means, do you?" she asked.

His hand was at his side, wrapped around his own knife. "Tell me."

She blinked in surprise, and pulled the sharp edge away from his skin, swinging it around so that its point was in the hollow of his throat.

"It means the Ryhmans won," she said. "We won the battle, not the war. It means that all that humans have to do is wait. Our Houses will fight each other. We will die. And with no one to replace us, we will be no more than a historical footnote."

"You don't know that."

"We can't be cloned and we are infertile," she said, spitting the last word out like a curse.

"There may be information on how to replicate the technology used to create us," he said. "That's why I saved the data core, the samples."

"And what if we can? What then? Will we make our own like slaves, growing them in tanks, like him," she said gesturing to the child at their feet. "Grow them to fight for us, as if they were nothing but meat to be fed into the grinder? Let them drown in their own waste? Abandon them to wild animals so they can be consumed like prey?"

She pulled the blade away from his throat, and tucked it into its sheath at her back. Pushing her sword aside, she moved back a few steps, and sank to the ground to cradle her head in her hands.

A distant hoot echoed through the still night. Wing flaps followed as a gentle breeze shook the distant trees and stirred the soft grass around their feet. Despite the distance she'd put between them, he could hear the raggedness of her breaths. It was as though drawing them, as though life itself had become too painful to bear.

"You're still weak," he said, rummaging through their supplies. He shoved a ration bar at her.

She threw it aside.

"I will force feed you," he said.

She raised her gaze to his. "I don't take my orders from you."

He had her on her back, arms pinned above her head, pressing the full weight of his body atop hers, his knee firmly planted between her legs, all before she took her next breath.

She struggled under him, twisting and straining, trying to push up using the injured leg he wasn't holding down. Her knee pounded into his back, but without the force needed to dislodge him. Her eyes were full of rage, her teeth bared, her cuspids a brilliant white against pink lips.

There was no longer a death's rattle to her breathing. It had been replaced with vicious purpose.

He smiled. This was the Teirani he'd grown up with, the Teirani he'd known.

"You really should've waited until you were fully healed and at full strength before challenging me, Teirani. You might have had a chance then."

Another venomous glare. One accompanied by a flutter of her carotid and the pure sweetness of arousal.

"Or is it defeat you're craving?" he asked. "Battle? Something, someone to fight? To pour all your pain into? Or to take it all away?"

Her eyes widened and color blazed in her cheeks. Color he didn't need his augmentations to see.

"You won't like me this way," she said through gritted teeth and made another futile attempt to dislodge him.

"And you won't be able to keep up the pretense of it for long. I smell nothing but invitation. A curious trait, don't you think, for an infertile species?"

"Another way for them to control us. To give us a taste of something we can't have."

"I think not," he said and kissed the pulse point at her neck. It doubled its pace.

He ran his aching cuspids up her arching neck. She'd become still but her heart was as loud as thunder, and if the blood rushing through her veins held any taint of fear, it was drowned out by arousal.

It was intoxicating.

With each breath he drew, every touch of lips, of tongue, to that silken skin, he could taste it. Feast on it. Take it all, knowing that no matter how much he had his fill, there would always be more. He eased up and she arched her back, then raised her head and captured his mouth with her own.

He let her wrists go and her hands fumbled with his belt as her tongue continued dueling with his. He took every bit of her anger, her rage.

It turned to a vibrant, pulsing tenderness that pierced his defenses in a way her rage had not. They might all eventually die. His subspecies might go extinct. But *he* would not be one of the ones that would die without ever having been alive.

By the time morning came, their lay in an exhausted pile, him curled around her, one hand cupping her breast, thumb scraping across the tightening nipple.

She pressed into him, casting a questioning gaze over her shoulder, a gaze that asked if he was ready to do battle again.

He was.

10

PYRE

*T*eirani dressed as Galeron repacked their dwindling supplies and their treasure.

There was a bite at the point where her neck met her shoulder, two precise incisions left by his cuspids. She ran her fingers over the healing bumps, then tugged the collar over them as if covering them would make what passed between them go away. The marks would fade soon enough, but for her, they'd always be there, a constant reminder of her surrender. Her submission. Her willing submission.

She'd bared her neck, drawn his head to it, and held him there, one hand anchored into his scalp, the other drawing encouraging furrows into his back.

She'd needed it. He'd needed it.

The need for it had been all-consuming, as if something dangerous and delightful, tender and powerful had woken within her. And when he'd sank those vestigial fangs into her flesh, thrusting into her at the same time, filling her again and again, the power of her orgasm had shattered her.

She shook her head.

Why had the humans that created them given them the ability to have sex, to enjoy it?

Why had they made it so that when Galeron took her, she felt fulfilled and complete, her mind, her heart, her world set aright?

All those years ago, every time they'd sparred, she had felt arousal's edge tugging at her core, twisting her emotions, driving her to best him while at the same time making her crave defeat. When it had all fallen apart she'd chosen Dynadin over Cadarn in no small part because she hadn't wanted to suffer the torment of being with him but not being able to be part of him.

And fate had thrust them together anyway.

They could spend the rest of their lives here, hide from their respective Houses, from any *donai* that might come. They could leave the chaos of House politics behind them, and revel in companionship and the emotion humans called love.

It wasn't even one of the emotions the *donai* were meant to have. For what use was a weapon that could fall in love, that could decide that another was more important than following orders?

Another as in lover. Another as in child.

She made her way to the gestation tank.

"Let me carry that for you, Teirani," Galeron said.

She shook her head. "No one is carrying him today."

He pulled her into an embrace, and kissed the top of her head.

"I'll gather the wood," he said, his voice just a bit ragged.

She nodded and waited for his scent to fade before opening the seal and dumping the liquid. It sluiced across the grass, red and black, and vile.

She took the baby in her arms, held him as a mother would.

"I'm sorry you never got the chance to live," she said, her voice shaking. "It's alright now. It's over. You are free and no one has dominion over you. No one can harm you anymore. No one can use you."

When Galeron returned, she was still holding the baby and humming. There were words to the song, words she could not recall. The melody would have to be enough.

Galeron built the pyre with trembling hands, casting sideways glances as her humming strangled with sobs.

"Are you ready?" he asked.

She looked down at that perfect button nose, those perfect little toes and fingers. The source of Avyanna's guilt crystalized in Teirani's heart: one did not have to bear a child to love him, to bear a burden, a responsibility, for his life. Or his death.

"Do you think we have souls?" she asked.

"Why wouldn't we?" Galeron asked. "We all started out as human. If humans have souls, we must as well."

"Do we have souls if we are never born?"

Wind stirred around them. Clouds had gathered and ozone filled the gusting air as it pulled angrily at the grass, driving it like tides sent to break themselves upon a shore.

"I don't know," he said.

"Lie to me."

"He had a soul, Teirani."

She handed the baby over. He barely filled Galeron's hands. She knew then, that no matter how hard she tried, she would never forget that image, that contrast of Galeron's strong, dark hands, holding the boy as if he were fragile and precious, as if he were, even in death, the most important person in the universe.

Galeron placed him on the pyre. She pulled off her jacket and draped it over the baby's tiny form, tucking it under him to keep the wind from snatching it and exposing him to nature's cruelty once again.

Waste not.

She would never wear that jacket again anyway. And it made a fitting shroud, with all its insignia. A little soldier he was, struggling to breathe, to live, even as technology and the people that made him failed him at every turn. Even as his own kind—as she—had failed him.

Just one. She'd wanted to save just one. It would have been a start, a small victory, one with a measure small enough to hold in her arms, her heart.

Galeron set a torch in her hand. Their gazes met.

He bent his head, touching his lips to her. It was chaste and sweet and somehow, full of promise.

She took a deep breath and thrust the torch into the kindling under the pyre. Her tiny soldier deserved a warrior's rites, a hero's pyre. Winds caught the flame and whipped them around, feeding the blaze.

By the time the sky joined her weeping, the tiny body was gone, reduced to ash.

11

FORMALITY

Galeron took Teirani's hand and held it as they left the pyre behind. The rain stopped as wind swept the storm away and the sky cleared to reveal twilight.

If he'd had any doubts about being in love, about his ability to fall in love, they had been erased. Not by the battle of wills, the duel fought with their passions, but by the image of Teirani holding that dead child as if it was her own. All his life, he and every *donai*, had been told two things—they could not love and they could not breed.

Nature would not be thwarted. They had been told this again and again.

They had been created to destroy and to die. Nothing more.

The rest—their passions, their desires, their ability to mimic human behaviors—were vestigial, like their cuspids, or their ears.

Yet nature had been thwarted. They had thwarted it last night, again and again. If they could only kill and die, then there was no reason to want to protect Teirani. She was not of his House. She wasn't part of his pack. And there was no reason to want to place a child—their child —in her arms, to fulfill a need neither of them were supposed to have.

Humans had made one fatal mistake when they'd made the *donai*.

They had put too much of themselves in their creations. Their fiddling with genetic codes, both human and non-human, had produced an error, an anomaly. The same anomaly that made him hold her hand, that made him never want to let it go. The same anomaly that made fire course through his veins whenever her tears or her sweat or her saliva touched him. The same anomaly that had made it impossible to resist the urge to bite her, to mark her, to possess her.

And he would not let her go. Not for any lord or liege or sovereign. Not by anyone's command. Vassals and their liege lords had duties and obligations to each other.

He was a vassal, not a slave. And a vassal—especially one that had done some great deed—could ask for a boon, one which his liege would have to grant.

Teirani was right in that no liege lord would take her oath if she betrayed her House.

He let her hand go and dropped the pack. She took two more steps before she turned, a puzzled frown on her face.

Their gazes met.

Galeron drew his sword.

Teirani drew hers.

"And if it's a draw?" she asked.

"It won't be."

She struck first, and again, drawing blood, moving in a blur.

But his reach was longer, the power behind his strikes, mightier, and his heart was in it in a way that hers could not be. For there was one thing he knew with certainty—she did not want him kneeling before her lord, his neck bare to her sword, upholding his honor by waiting for the finishing blow.

He knew it with as much certainty as he'd known that when she'd bared her neck for him, it had been so he could mark her as his.

The swords were, as always, mere formality.

NEWSLETTER SIGNUP

Be in the know! Be the first to know!

Sign up for my newsletter and get the latest news, releases, and maybe some freebies.

Click here to sign up or go to www.monalisafoster.com

AFTERWORD

In the spring of 2017 I was part of a writer's workshop that included the chance to sell stories for six different anthologies.

Dominion was originally written for a romance anthology. However, it was bought by Ron and Bridget Collins for their **Face the Strange** anthology. The coronapocalypse delayed the publication until 2020. By then I had already written the first novel, **Ravages of Honor**, and several other shorter works in the same universe.

I am thrilled to bring *Dominion* to you as a standalone. It allowed me to further explore the origins of the *donai*, something that I was still fleshing out in 2017.

Like all of my works, *Dominion* and its companion works are all complete, standalone works, with a beginning, middle, and end.

There are no cliffhangers.

You do not need to read any of the short stories or novellas in order for them to make sense.

ABOUT THE AUTHOR

Monalisa won life's lottery when she escaped communism and became an unhyphenated American citizen. Her works tend to explore themes of freedom, liberty, and personal responsibility. Despite her degree in physics, she's worked in several fields including engineering and medicine. She and her husband are living their happily ever after in Texas.

She learned English by reading and translating books from the juvenile section at the public library. She'd walk to the library with her dictionary and a notebook and start copying sentences and then translating them by hand.

After a few days of this, a kindly librarian took pity on her and offered her a library card and then broke some rules in issuing one to a ten-year-old. This was back in the bad old days when kids were still free range and parents didn't get jailed for letting them go places unsupervised. But, the library was air conditioned, an important thing when the temperature reaches triple digits, so she spent the summer there anyway, and along the way discovered Robert Heinlein and science fiction. It didn't take long to devour the juvenile section and move on to the grown-up books.

www.monalisafoster.com

facebook.com/MonalisaFosterStoryteller

twitter.com/HouseDobromil

amazon.com/Monalisa-Foster/B075Z7SDJ1

pinterest.com/m2foster

bookbub.com/authors/m2foster

goodreads.com/m2foster

instagram.com/monalisa_foster_storyteller

RAVAGES OF HONOR READING ORDER

- Bonds of Love and Duty: A Short Story
- Dominion: A Ravages of Honor Novella
- Enemy Beloved: A Ravages of Honor Novella
- Featherlight: A Ravages of Honor Novella
- Ravages of Honor: Conquest (Book 1)
- Ravages of Honor: Ascension (Book 2)

RAVAGES OF HONOR: CONQUEST
(BOOK 1)

What would you do to save your world?

Syteria was kidnapped as a child. The Rhoans enslaved her, brainwashed and masculinized her in order to turn her into a soldier against her will. Despite this, she has not forgotten who or what she is. It's why she can't pull the trigger and kill her brother. She turns rogue in order to save him and his family, knowing that it will cost her everything.

But when the ship taking her to her execution is pulled through space and time, she finds herself a stranger in a strange land, reborn into a new body, the one she would have grown into had the Rhoans not changed her.

Darien, the half-breed prince of a noble House, serves out the last days of his term of exile for defying his emperor. When an alien ship appears out of a wormhole, he can't resist going after it, no matter the price. He rescues the derelict spaceship's only survivor, a barely warm corpse he doesn't even realize is a woman.

His motives are suspect, especially when turning Syteria over to the tender mercies of the Imperium would cost him nothing and redeem him in the eyes of the emperor. Cultures and passions clash in this epic adventure featuring galactic empires, feuding noble houses, and court intrigues.

Ravages of Honor: Conquest is an Outlander in space with genetic engineering, nanotech, and swords. First in a series, with a complete story that can be read as a standalone.

ENEMY BELOVED: A RAVAGES OF HONOR NOVELLA

Ilithyia Dayasagar survives alone, on a distant continent. For her mission to succeed, she must remain hidden.

But the fireball that splits the sky and scorches the earth does not go unnoticed. Neither does the corpse she finds instead of the meteor.

Especially once he turns out to be very much alive. And very much a mystery.

Passion and betrayal collide in "Enemy Beloved," a story of true love and sacrifice.[1]

Available exclusively for newsletter subscribers via www.monalisafoster.com.

---

1. A shorter version of this novella appeared in the Venus Anthology.

FEATHERLIGHT: A RAVAGES OF HONOR NOVELLA

Lady Valeria Yedon, the emperor's favorite assassin, thought herself free.

But in the Imperium, oaths of fealty have no expiration date. The burdens of duty and honor bind every-thing, and everyone, together.

And freedom always comes at a price.

Part of the **Ravages of Honor** universe, "Featherlight" focuses on one warrior's struggle for her future...and her soul.

BONDS OF LOVE AND DUTY: A RAVAGES OF HONOR SHORT STORY

Available April 7, 2020

Mankind made a crucial mistake by creating the *donai*. Now its about to make another—one from which it may never recover.

For fifty years, Calyce has fulfilled the role of mother to the *donai* children under her care. Determined to save as many as possible, she comes up with a plan.

Andret cannot wait to start his formal military training. Calyce has raised him well. He would do anything for her.

Bonds of Love and Duty focuses on the early events leading to the *donai* rebellion against their human creators.[1]

---

1. "Bonds of Duty and Love" is a short story in this anthology edited by Laurell K. Hamilton and William McCaskey.

PRETENDING TO SLEEP: A COMMUNISM SURVIVOR'S SHORT STORY

Based on actual events, this short story provides a quick glimpse into life under Ceaucescu's brutal communist regime. Like so many Romanians, ten-year-old Renata lives in fear of Securitate (Ceaucescu's secret police). They don't always take you in the middle of the night. In a world where the living envy the dead, not all examples are made in the shadows. Some are made in the light of day.

(This book is appropriate for children 10 years and older.)

CATCHING THE DARK

Operation Barbarossa destroyed most of the Tsarina Tatiana Romanova's aircraft.

Sixteen-year-old Natalya loves to fly, to soar. And now she gets to. As the youngest member of the Tsarina's Own Night Bomber regiment.

A story for anyone who loves WW2 alt-history, aviation, and stories about heroism.

Night Witches strike terror in the hearts of darkness.[1]

---

1. "Catching the Dark" was first published in the anthology, **To Slip the Surly Bonds** (edited by Chris Kennedy and James Young).

PROMETHEA INVICTA

Promethea Invicta: A Novella

No longer part of the United States, in 2071 the Sovereign Republic of Texas remains bound by the Outer Space Treaty it inherited.

Theia Rhodos stands ready to free humanity from the shackles that keep lunar resources out of her reach. Done taking "no" for an answer, she acts boldly, ready to sacrifice everything.

Only the gods of scarcity, woe and lament stand in her way.

Everything in life has a cost. And a price.

9 798201 430412